Who Broke
Lincoln's Thumb?

by Ron Roy
illustrated by Timothy Bush

A STEPPING STONE BOOK™

Random House 🏠 New York

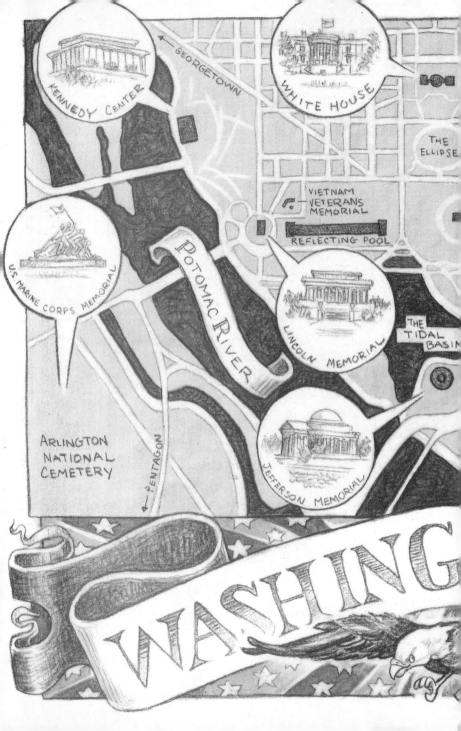

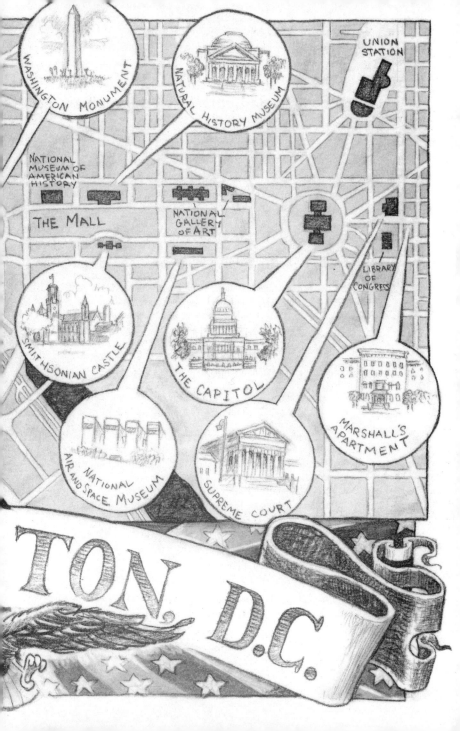

This book is dedicated to Bo Sanchez.
—R.R.

Photo credits: pp. 88–89 courtesy of the Library of Congress.

www.randomhouse.com/kids
www.steppingstonesbooks.com

Library of Congress Cataloging-in-Publication Data
Roy, Ron.
Who broke Lincoln's thumb? / by Ron Roy ; illustrated by Timothy Bush. — 1st ed.
    p.   cm. — (Capital mysteries ; #5)
"A Stepping Stone Book."
SUMMARY: When they discover that one of the thumbs has been broken off the statue in the Lincoln Memorial, KC and Marshall set out to learn what happened and restore the thumb before a ceremony honoring the sculptor.
ISBN 0-375-82558-4 (pbk.) — ISBN 0-375-92558-9 (lib. bdg.)
[1. Lost and found possessions—Fiction. 2. Lincoln Memorial (Washington, D.C.)—Fiction. 3. Statues—Fiction. 4. Washington (D.C.)—Fiction. 5. Mystery and detective stories.] I. Bush, Timothy, ill. II. Title. III. Series.
PZ7.R8139Wk 2005 [Fic]—dc22   2004027362

Printed in the United States of America
First Edition 10 9 8 7 6 5 4 3 2 1

Contents

1

Did You Lose Something, President Lincoln?

"So do I have to call you Miss Corcoran now?" Marshall Li asked his friend KC Corcoran. KC's mom had married President Zachary Thornton, and KC was now living in the White House.

KC and Marshall were walking toward the Lincoln Memorial.

"No, you can still call me KC," she said. "But don't forget to bow every time you see me."

Marshall laughed. Then something caught his eye. He squatted down in front of a rosebush. "Wow, look at that!" he cried. A fat black and yellow spider was

1

dangling from its web in the bush.

"No thanks!" KC said. "You look at it for me!"

"But he's so beautiful," Marshall said, inching closer to the spider. He loved most animals, but especially the kinds with six or eight legs. Marshall dreamed of getting a job in the insect room at the Museum of Natural History.

KC pulled him back. "Come on, Marsh, before it decides to rain again."

The morning had started out cloudy, and then the sky had turned black. Wind had howled through Washington, D.C., and large raindrops had pelted down.

By ten o'clock, the rain had stopped. The sun broke through the clouds as KC and Marshall crossed the lawn near the Reflecting Pool. Gusts of wind blew leaves all around their feet.

"I don't understand why you need to take pictures of Abraham Lincoln's statue," Marshall said. They had reached the wide lawn in front of the Memorial.

"I told you on the phone this morning," KC said. "But you were feeding Spike and you weren't paying attention."

Spike was Marshall's pet tarantula, who slept inside a baseball cap in Marshall's room.

"So tell me again," Marshall said, grinning. "I promise to listen!"

"Mr. Alubicki told us to do a report on a famous person, right?" KC asked.

"Right," Marshall said. "I'm doing mine on Spider-Man."

KC looked at him in amazement. "Marshall, Spider-Man is a comic-book character, not a real person," she said.

Marshall grinned. "Mr. A didn't say the person had to be real. Spider-Man is definitely famous!"

"Well, mine will be about Daniel Chester French," KC said.

"Who's he?" Marshall asked as they walked toward the Lincoln Memorial.

"A famous sculptor! He sculpted Abraham Lincoln's statue," KC said. "It took him four years!" She reached into her backpack and pulled out her new digital camera, a gift from the president.

"How do you know all this stuff?" Marshall asked.

KC planned to become a TV anchor-woman someday. Her hobby was memorizing a lot of facts.

"I read a lot about him in the newspaper,"

KC said. "The president has declared today Daniel Chester French Day. There was a big article about the ceremony at five o'clock tonight."

"Will there be cake and ice cream?" asked Marshall.

"Probably," KC said, nodding toward the Lincoln Memorial. "Look, isn't that prettier than some hairy old spider?"

Now that the storm had passed, people were on the lawn in front of the Lincoln Memorial enjoying the day. A couple of little kids were trying to fly a kite, but the wind kept crashing it to the ground. Two young men were tossing a Frisbee back and forth.

KC and Marshall climbed the wide steps and walked between the columns in front of the Lincoln statue. They stared up at Lincoln's calm face, high above them. Daniel Chester French had sculpted him sitting in a big chair, which stood on top of a ten-foot platform.

An aluminum ladder leaned against the platform. A black ladder lay on the floor next to two buckets of cleaning supplies.

"I read that the statue is nineteen feet high from Lincoln's feet to the top of his head," KC told Marshall. "And if Lincoln could stand up, he'd be twenty-eight feet tall!"

A man and woman were standing in front of the statue with a little kid who was sucking his thumb. The man was snapping pictures. The camera's flash blazed each time the shutter clicked.

Suddenly the man pulled his camera away from his face. He stared at the statue, then said, "I don't believe it!"

"What?" the woman asked.

The man pointed upward toward Lincoln's left hand. "His thumb is gone!" the man said.

KC and Marshall rushed forward. "Oh my gosh!" KC cried. "One of his thumbs *is* missing!"

Where Lincoln's left thumb should have been, there was just a stump.

The man grinned down at his son. "That's what happens when people suck their thumbs," he joked.

"Do you suppose the thumb just fell off?" the woman asked.

"If it did, it should be here," the man said, glancing down at the area near the statue. "But it's not."

"Come on, Daddy," the little boy said.

"You promised we could see the Air and Space Museum!"

The family hurried away, passing two men coming up the steps. One was tall and skinny. The other was short and stumpy, like a fire hydrant.

They were wearing gray work shirts with NATIONAL PARK SERVICE stitched over the pockets.

"Did you come about Lincoln's thumb?" KC asked when the men reached the statue.

"What thumb?" the tall man asked.

Marshall pointed up to Lincoln's left hand. "That thumb, only it's gone," he said.

Both men stood under the statue gazing up.

"Well, I'll be darned," said the tall man. "It was here a while ago, wasn't it, Stub?"

The man named Stub nodded. "Righto, Ralphie. When I dusted his hands, Abe had both his thumbs," he said.

"Why did you dust him?" KC asked.

"We're cleaning the statue for the ceremony tonight," Stub answered. "We just took a little coffee break. When we left, he still had his thumb!"

Ralphie pulled a snapshot out of his pocket and handed it to KC. "Some tourist took this and gave it to me," he said.

KC and Marshall looked at the picture. In it, Stub was standing on the black ladder with a dusting cloth in one hand. The ladder was up on the platform, leaning against Lincoln's right knee.

KC and Marshall could easily see that Lincoln still had both his thumbs.

2

Mr. President, We Have a Problem

"Do you mind if I go up on your ladders for a minute?" KC asked. "I want to see that hand close up."

Ralphie shook his head. "Sorry, miss," he said. "We could get in trouble for letting a civilian use our equipment."

"I'm not exactly a regular civilian," KC said. "My mother is married to President Thornton."

Both men gawked at KC.

"You're that kid?" Stub asked. "The First Daughter?"

KC nodded. "I'm KC Corcoran," she said with a big smile. "And if you let me climb up there, I'll tell the president how helpful you were."

"Okay, miss, I guess it'll be all right," Ralphie said. He climbed up onto the platform and stood next to Lincoln's feet.

Stub lifted the black ladder off the floor and handed it up. Ralphie leaned the ladder against Lincoln's right knee.

"Okay, come on up, miss, but be careful," Ralphie said, looking down at KC.

Stub held the lower ladder for her, and KC scampered up with her camera strap around her wrist. Then she climbed up the black ladder. At the top, her nose was only inches from Lincoln's left hand.

"What do you see?" Marshall asked.

"It looks like the thumb broke off," KC said.

"KC, what do you mean? We *know* the

thumb broke off," Marshall said.

"I mean, I don't think it was cut off, like with a saw or something," KC said. "Hey, there's a red mark here, right near where it broke!"

"What kind of red mark?" Marshall asked.

KC looked closely at the strange red mark on the white marble. She gently touched it with her finger. "I can't tell what it is," she said. "Just red."

KC snapped a picture. "Okay, I'm coming down!" she called over her shoulder.

A minute later, she was standing next to Marshall.

"Thanks a lot," she told Stub and Ralphie.

"Can I have my picture back?" Ralphie asked.

"Oh, can I keep it for now?" KC asked. "I'm sure the president will want to see it. He might send you a thank-you note."

"Okay!" Ralphie said with a big smile.

KC and Marshall raced toward the White House.

Twenty minutes later, they rushed through the private entrance. Out of breath, they hurried down the corridor to the president's living quarters. A tall marine guard stood at attention next to the door.

"Hi, Arnold," the kids said.

The marine looked down at them. "Hi, guys. What's up?"

Marshall said, "Lincoln's thumb is—"

"Nine inches long!" KC interrupted. She gave Marshall a look.

Arnold smiled at KC. "How do you

happen to know that?" he asked.

"I'm studying the Lincoln Memorial," she said. "Are my mom and the president in?"

Arnold nodded and opened the door for the kids.

They hurried inside and ran toward the library, where the president liked to relax.

"Why'd you stop me?" Marshall asked KC. "The missing thumb is huge news! If I don't tell someone, I'll bust open!"

"I know, but the president should hear about it first," KC said as they stepped into the library.

"Hear about what?" the president asked.

President Zachary Thornton was sitting on a sofa next to KC's mom, Lois. They were both practically buried in lists for the big celebration that night.

George, the president's cat, was lying in the middle of the mess of papers.

"Okay, Marsh, now you can tell him," KC said.

"We were at the Lincoln Memorial!" Marshall blurted out. "And guess what happened!"

"We won't have to guess if you tell us," KC's mom said, smiling at her daughter's best friend.

"One of Lincoln's thumbs is missing!" Marshall nearly shouted.

The president and First Lady stared at the two kids.

"His thumb . . . ," the president said.

"Is missing?" his wife added.

"Honest, Mom," KC said. "We went to take pictures for my report on Daniel

Chester French. When we got there, Lincoln's left thumb was gone!"

The president blinked. "Just . . . gone? Like, broken off?" he asked.

KC nodded. "There's just a short stump now," she said.

The four stared at each other. Finally, the president jumped from the sofa and hurried out of the room. George the cat meowed and hopped down to the floor.

"Sit, kids," KC's mom said. She made room on the sofa. "This isn't a joke, is it?" she asked. "You're not just teasing, are you?"

"Cross my heart!" Marshall said.

"I even took a picture," KC said. She pulled her camera from her pack. She clicked a button, and the image of Lincoln's left hand with its missing thumb showed up in the small screen.

"Oh my," KC's mom breathed. The picture clearly showed that Lincoln's left hand had no thumb.

KC's mom held the camera closer. "What's that little red mark?" she asked.

"I don't know," KC said. "I looked at it, but—"

"The Park Service is on the case," the president said as he hurried back into the room. "A couple of park rangers were cleaning the statue this morning. Maybe they saw what happened."

"We already talked to them!" Marshall said. "They said the thumb was there earlier this morning."

"They let me climb up on their ladders," KC said. "They gave me this." She produced the picture of Stub on the black ladder next to Lincoln's knee.

"KC took this one," Lois said. She passed the camera to the president.

The president sat and studied both pictures. In the Polaroid snapshot, Lincoln had both thumbs. In KC's digital picture, there was just a broken stub where the left thumb should have been.

The president set the camera on the coffee table and placed the snapshot next to it. "Perfect," he muttered, glancing at the tall clock standing in the corner. "At five o'clock, hundreds of people will be gathered on the Memorial's steps to admire Daniel Chester French's most famous statue."

President Thornton turned pale. "And I'll have to tell them all that someone broke off Lincoln's thumb!"

3

The Red Runaround

"Maybe Marsh and I can find the thumb," KC suggested. "We have over five hours."

"That's a nice idea, honey," KC's mom said. "But how? Where would you look?"

"There were a lot of people near the Memorial when we got there," KC said. "Maybe one of them noticed something."

"But we don't even know when the thumb was taken," the president said.

"Yes, we do!" Marshall said. He flipped over the photograph KC had gotten from Ralphie. On the back was the date and the time the photo was taken. "See, this was taken at 10:07 this morning and the thumb was still there."

KC grabbed her camera and found her digital picture. "Look, there's the time!" she said, pointing at the corner of the image. "I snapped this one at 10:37!"

The president sat up. "So the thumb vanished in the half hour between 10:07 and 10:37!"

KC leaped off the sofa. "Come on! Maybe we can find people who were at the Memorial during that time!" she said.

The president stood up, too. "I'll talk to the FBI!" he said, rushing from the room.

"I'll call the National Park Service!" Lois said, reaching for the telephone.

Marshall rubbed his stomach. "I'll have a sandwich," he said.

"We don't get lunch until Lincoln gets

his thumb back!" KC said, dragging Marshall from his seat.

By the time KC and Marshall reached the Lincoln Memorial again, the wide lawn in front was crowded. People were sunbathing and eating snacks on the steps and near the Reflecting Pool.

Hot dog and ice cream vendors were doing a brisk business. One man was selling balloons with Lincoln's face on them.

"Look," Marshall said.

KC peered through the columns. She could see a man up on a ladder examining Lincoln's left hand. Down below, Ralphie and Stub were talking with a man and woman in business suits. Two official-looking black cars were parked nearby.

Yellow crime-scene tape was tied to

two of the columns, keeping people away from the Lincoln statue.

"There were some kids with a kite here before," Marshall said, "but I don't see them now."

Suddenly a Frisbee zipped past KC's face. A man leaped up, plucked the Frisbee out of the air, and whipped it back to his friend.

"I remember those guys!" KC said. "Let's go talk to them."

As KC and Marshall walked over to the Frisbee throwers, one of them missed a catch. The wind took the Frisbee up into a tree, where it got stuck in the branches.

"Good one, Max," the taller guy said.

"I can get it, Joker," Max replied.

Joker and Max walked over to the tree. Joker bent over, and Max climbed onto his marble thumb?" KC asked.

arshall looked at KC. "You think
two guys did it?" he asked.

C nodded. "Their Frisbee was doing
fifty miles an hour," she said. "And
l. That mark I saw on Lincoln's hand
have been red plastic!"

aybe," Marshall said. "But if their
broke the thumb, why would they
hanging around? Wouldn't they
?"

h, I guess you're right," KC said.

noticed a woman sitting a few feet
ading a book. But then she put it
d took a bottle of nail polish from
ket. The woman began painting
er long nails.

ared. The polish was bright red.
ooted a little closer. She tipped

shoulders to grab the Frisbee out of the branches. Then he jumped to the ground as nimble as a monkey.

"Hi," KC said to the man called Max. "Could I ask you something?"

"Sure, what's up, kid?" Max said. He had muscular arms and wore a baggy George Washington University sweatshirt.

"Did you hear about Lincoln's thumb?" KC asked.

Max grinned at her, spinning the red Frisbee on one finger. "What is this, a joke?" he asked. "Okay, I give up. What about Lincoln's thumb?"

"It's not a joke," Marshall said.

"Sounds like one to me," Joker said. He was much taller than Max and wore his hair in a bright yellow buzz cut.

KC explained about the missing

thumb. "We wondered
one sneaking around th

Joker grinned. "I g
be thumbing rides an

"Seriously, we did
Memorial," Max saic
on our game."

Max held out
Someone had prin
black marker.

"Come on, roor
to his tall friend.
French test."

The two me
toward the stree
dered back tow;

"What shou
asked as they s

"Do you th

off a

M
those
KC
about
it's re
could

"M
Frisbe
still be
take of

"Yea
KC
away, re
down an
her poc
one of h
KC st
KC sc

her head so she could read the book's title. It said TEN WAYS TO GET RICH FAST.

"Excuse me," KC said to the woman. "Did you hear about Lincoln's thumb?"

The woman smiled. Her bright red lips matched the nail polish. A name tag on her blouse said FIONA ROBB. "I sure did!" she said. "I work in the bookstore here inside the Memorial. Some tourists were talking about it. Some joker probably stole the thing as a souvenir."

Fiona blew on her fingernail, being careful not to touch the wet polish. Then she put away her polish, grabbed her book, and stood up. "Gotta get back to work," she said, and zipped up the steps.

When she was gone, KC grabbed Marshall by the arm. "What if the mark I saw is red nail polish?" KC asked with her eyes dancing. "Fiona could have stolen Lincoln's thumb!"

Marshall looked at her. "Why would she do that?" he asked.

"She was reading a book about how to get rich," KC said. "She could be planning to sell the thumb!"

"Who would buy it?" Marshall asked.

"Are you kidding?" KC said. "Lincoln's thumb is valuable!"

"How would she climb up to get it?" Marshall asked.

"On the ladders, like I did," KC said.

Marshall shook his head. "Ralphie and Stub would never let her," he said.

"But they left the ladders there when they took their break," KC insisted. "They wouldn't have seen her climb them!"

"I vote for Max and Joker," Marshall

said. "They wouldn't even need a ladder. Max could stand on Joker's shoulders to get at the thumb."

"Maybe it wasn't Fiona or those Frisbee guys," KC said suddenly. "Look down there by the Reflecting Pool."

Marsh looked. He saw a bunch of tourists taking pictures of a man on stilts. The man was dressed as Abraham Lincoln in a black top hat and a beard.

"So?" Marshall said. "He's around a lot. He charges a dollar to take his picture."

"I know," KC said. "I saw him here earlier, too. But check out the stilts, Marsh."

Marshall looked, then gulped. The stilts were as red as a fire engine.

4

The Color of Clues

Marshall and KC sat on the steps and stared at the man on the red stilts. "Are you thinking what I'm thinking?" KC asked.

Marshall nodded. "Yup. That guy wouldn't have to climb on anything to get to Lincoln's hand!" he said.

"Yeah, he could reach up with one of his stilts and smack the thumb off," KC said. "The red paint on the stilt could have left that mark I saw."

KC skipped down the steps and Marshall followed her. She handed her camera to her friend and pulled a dollar bill from a wallet in her pack.

"Take my picture with him," KC whispered as they approached the man.

"Why?" he asked.

"You'll see," KC said mysteriously.

KC and Marshall walked over to the man on stilts. He glanced down at them. "Want a picture with Honest Abe?" he asked.

"Yes, I do!" KC said. She posed between the stilts, hoping the man didn't notice as she pulled her Swiss Army knife from her pack.

Marshall backed up so he could get KC and the man in the picture. "Okay, one, two, three, say *pizza!*" he said.

As Marshall snapped the picture, KC scraped a tiny curl of red paint from one of the stilts. She slipped the knife and

paint sample into a pocket. Then she handed up the dollar bill.

"Thanks, kids," the man on stilts said.

"Thank you, too!" KC said.

More people approached the man on stilts as KC and Marshall walked away.

"Okay, I saw that," Marshall said. "Why did you steal a piece of his stilt?"

"I wanted a sample of that red paint," KC said. "And I got it! Now we can see if it's the same as the red mark on Lincoln's hand."

"Okay, but what about the red nail polish and the red Frisbee?" Marshall said. "How are you gonna get those samples?"

"I'm not sure," KC said. She looked at her watch. "Gosh, we only have four hours to get the thumb back!"

"Less than that," Marshall said. "Even

if we find the thumb, it'll take some time to attach it to Lincoln's hand again." He giggled. "I wonder if superglue would work."

"Funny," KC said. "Come on, let's hit the bookstore first."

KC and Marshall raced back up the stone steps. Ralphie and Stub and their ladders were gone. The two black cars were gone, too. The yellow crime-scene tape was still wrapped around the columns.

In the corner to the right of the Lincoln statue was a small bookstore. KC and Marshall walked in and looked around. A few people wandered among the rows of books.

KC bumped Marshall's shoulder. "There she is!" she whispered.

Fiona was sitting on a stool behind the counter. Her book, *Ten Ways to Get Rich Fast*, was opened and she was reading.

KC marched over to the counter. "Hi," she said. "I was wondering if you could do me a favor."

Fiona looked up. She recognized KC and Marshall. "Like what?" she asked.

"I want to get my mom a gift, and I think she'd like your nail polish," KC said. "Could I see it again?"

Fiona held up her hands, wiggling her ten red fingernails. "It's called Racy Red," she said. "Would you like me to paint one of your nails so you can show it to your mom?"

"Great, thanks!" KC said, holding out her left hand. "How about doing my thumb?"

"Thumb it is," Fiona said. She pulled out the bottle and unscrewed the top.

KC watched as her thumbnail became Racy Red.

"It takes a few minutes to dry," Fiona said. "Don't touch anything or it'll smear."

"Thanks a lot!" KC said. Waving her thumb in the air, she yanked Marshall toward the exit.

"Now we have two samples," KC said.

"Pretty sneaky," Marshall said. "But those two Frisbee guys won't be as easy!"

"We'll think of something," KC said, checking her watch again.

5

The Snoring Suspect

The day had turned warmer. Hundreds of people were sitting on the lawn, lunching and enjoying the sun. As KC and Marshall walked, they kept their eyes peeled for Joker and Max.

They spotted a lot of men with Frisbees, but none had a bright yellow buzz cut.

When they reached the Washington Monument, Marshall suddenly stopped. "Wait a minute, I just thought of something!" he said.

"Tell me," KC said, glancing at her watch.

"One of the guys playing Frisbee was wearing a sweatshirt with GEORGE WASHINGTON UNIVERSITY printed on the front!" he said.

"You're right!" KC said. "He said he had to go study for a French test, so he must be a student. Maybe we can find them on campus!"

She and Marshall raced toward Constitution Avenue. KC waved at a taxi and the driver pulled over. The kids jumped in the back. "Do you know how to get to George Washington University?" KC asked the driver.

"I sure do. My girlfriend goes there," the young driver said. "The campus is over on G Street."

He zoomed back into traffic.

"How are we supposed to find them?"

Marshall asked KC. "There are probably thousands of students there!"

The driver glanced into his rearview mirror. "Who are you looking for?" he asked.

"Their names are Max and Joker," KC explained. "Joker is tall and he has bright yellow hair."

The driver shook his head. "Tell you what. I'll drop you off at the office for student housing," he said. "They might know these guys."

A few minutes later, the driver guided his cab through two brick columns. On one was a plaque reading GEORGE WASHINGTON UNIVERSITY.

The driver stopped in front of a small white building. KC paid the fare and gave him a tip.

As the cab sped away, KC checked her watch. "We have three and a half hours," she said.

They hurried up to the shiny black door. In the center was a small sign that said STUDENT HOUSING OFFICE. PLEASE COME IN.

KC stopped and looked at Marshall. "We don't know their last names," she said. "How will we ever find them?"

"We know they're Max and Joker," Marshall said. "Maybe that'll be enough."

KC shook her head. "This is a big school," she said. She began pacing.

"Wait a minute," Marshall said. "I saw J.K. written on their Frisbee. Maybe Joker is a nickname and his real name is something else!"

KC stared at Marshall. She closed her

eyes. "Joker. . . . Jo . . . ker," she mumbled. Her eyes popped open. "Maybe his name is Joe Kerr!"

"It's worth a try," Marshall said.

He opened the door and they walked into an office. Three workers sat at computers, typing and talking into headsets.

One man noticed KC and Marshall and looked up from his keyboard. "Can I help you?" he asked.

"We're looking for two students," KC said. "Their names are Max and Joker, but Joker might be a nickname. His real name could be Joe Kerr."

"He has yellow hair in a buzz cut," Marshall added. "And they're room-mates."

The man typed something, clicked the mouse, then smiled. "Yes, Maxwell

Perkins and Joseph Kerr. They share a room at Jefferson Hall."

He pulled a map from a pile on the counter and drew circles around two buildings.

"You're here," he said, pointing to one of the circles. "Take this path to Jefferson. It's two minutes away."

The kids thanked him and followed the map. Jefferson Hall was a brick building shaded by trees. A guy reading on the front steps knew Max and Joker. "They live in room 10, in the back," he said, moving so they could get to the front door.

They walked down a dim hallway. Most of the doors were open, so KC and Marshall could see students sleeping or studying. Music was playing in some of the rooms.

Room 10 was the last one on the hall-way. There was no music, but KC heard snoring. She crept up to the door and peeked into the room.

A fan sat on a bureau, making a low hum. Joker lay sprawled on his bed with an arm covering his eyes. A French book rested on his stomach.

Max was snoring on the other bed. His hands were crossed over his chest. And beneath those big hands lay the red Frisbee.

KC backed away from the door.

"Now what?" Marshall whispered.

"We have to get that Frisbee!" KC hissed right back.

"Well, I'm not waking him up," Marshall said.

They stood outside the door listening

to Max's snoring and the whirring of the fan.

Suddenly KC grinned. She tiptoed into the room, walked over to the fan, and switched it to HIGH. Then she turned the fan so it was aimed right at Max's face.

At first, Max didn't do anything. Then suddenly he sprang up like a jack-in-the-box.

KC and Marshall dropped to the floor. KC held her breath. Her heart was beating so fast she was sure Max could hear it! But nothing happened, so she peeked up over the edge of Max's bed.

With his eyes still closed, Max was pulling a blanket over his legs. The Frisbee rolled onto the floor.

KC snatched it up and dashed out

of the room. Marshall was inches behind her.

KC stopped halfway down the hall. She had a big grin on her face.

"KC, you just stole that guy's Frisbee!" Marshall said.

"I didn't steal it!" KC said, fumbling inside her backpack. "I just borrowed it for a minute."

The Frisbee was old and battered. The edges had been ripped and cracked from smacking into things. KC peeled off a tiny piece of the red plastic and put it into her pack.

Then she walked quickly back to the room and left the Frisbee on the floor just inside the door. Max and Joker were still sleeping.

Marshall followed KC outside. The

man on the steps looked up. "Did you find them?" he asked.

"Yeah, but they were asleep, so we didn't disturb them," KC said. She and Marshall hurried away from Jefferson Hall.

At the street, KC waved for a cab. A green one pulled up, and KC yanked open the rear door.

"Take us to the White House as fast as you can!" she yelled.

6
The $100,000 Thumb

"You two are awesome!" the President of the United States said.

KC and Marshall blushed.

Yvonne, the president's maid, was preparing sandwiches and lemonade for lunch.

The kids had returned to the White House and rushed into the president's private kitchen. They quickly told the president and KC's mom about meeting Max and Joker, Fiona, and the man on red stilts.

On the kitchen table, three tiny red items lay on a paper towel.

One was a curl of red paint from the wooden stilt.

The second was the tiny piece of plastic KC had peeled from the Frisbee.

The third item was a clipping from KC's thumbnail painted Racy Red.

"How did you manage to get these?" KC's mom asked.

Before KC could answer, Mary Kincaid, the vice president, stuck her head through the door. "Ms. Pierce is here," she told the president.

"Thanks, Mary. Please show her in," the president said.

A moment later, a tall woman entered the kitchen. She wore blue coveralls with FBI printed on the back.

"Thank you for coming so quickly," the president said. He introduced Lois and the kids to Ms. Pierce, a scientist with the FBI.

"My pleasure, Mr. President. Are those the samples, sir?" Ms. Pierce asked, nodding toward the paper towel.

"Yes," said the president. "Please compare them with the red mark KC saw on Lincoln's left hand. Let me know what you find immediately!"

"Yes, sir!" Ms. Pierce hurried away with the samples.

"How long will it take her to find out?" Marshall asked.

"Probably not long at all, once she compares them," the president said. "I have other FBI staff watching Fiona and the two college boys and the man on stilts. As soon as we get the word from Ms. Pierce, an arrest will be made."

They were all in the library eating brownies when the phone rang twenty minutes later. The president put down his milk to answer it. "Yes, I see. Thank you very much, Ms. Pierce," he said before hanging up.

Everyone stared at the president.

"Which one is it?" KC asked.

"That red mark did not come from nail polish or Frisbee plastic or a painted stilt," the president said. "It was made by something else entirely."

"What was it?" his wife asked.

"Ms. Pierce said the mark is some kind of red paper with glue on one side," the president said. "She'll do a more thorough study in her lab. But I'm afraid we won't get the thumb back in time for the celebration."

Everyone looked up at the clock.

The ceremony would begin in two hours.

"I'll go change my speech," the president said, shaking his head in disgust. "The Lincoln statue will never be the same."

Just then Mary Kincaid burst into the room. "Sir, I just received this!" she blurted. She was holding a piece of paper and an envelope.

"Mary, what's the matter?" the president asked.

She passed him the paper. "It's a ransom note," she said. "For Lincoln's thumb!"

The president placed the paper on the coffee table.

Everyone read the note silently.

WE HAVE THE THUMB. YOU CAN HAVE IT BACK FOR $100,000. PUT THE MONEY IN A GARBAGE BAG. LEAVE THE BAG IN THE TRASH CAN ON THE SOUTHEAST CORNER OF THE REFLECTING POOL. MAKE THE DROP AT EXACTLY FOUR O'CLOCK! WE'LL BE WATCHING. IF YOU SEND COPS, THE THUMB DIS-APPEARS FOREVER!

"I can't believe this is happening!" President Thornton shouted. "Whoever heard of holding a thumb hostage?"

"Why four o'clock?" Marshall asked.

"These thieves are smart," the president said. "They picked a time when there would be thousands of tourists around the Reflecting Pool. No one will notice them pick up the money."

"What are you going to do, Zachary?" Lois asked quietly.

The president shook his head. "Pay the ransom. I don't have a choice," he mumbled as he left the room.

Mary Kincaid picked up the ransom note by its edges. "Maybe they left fingerprints," she said, then followed the president.

KC's mom let out a sigh. "What are you kids going to do?" she asked, walking to the door. "I have to be with Zachary."

"Finish these brownies," Marshall said, reaching for one.

"We'll be fine, Mom," KC said. Her mother nodded and went to find the president.

KC began pacing in front of Marshall. "Did you notice that the ransom note said 'we'?" she asked. "So it wasn't just one person who stole the thumb."

"Maybe it was that man with his wife and kid," Marshall said. "Remember, he was taking pictures when we first got there this morning."

"Marsh, he's the one who told *us* the thumb was missing," KC said.

She reached for the snapshot of Stub on the ladder at 10:07. Lincoln still had his thumb.

KC's picture, taken a half hour later, showed no thumb.

KC tapped the snapshot of Stub standing on the black ladder. "Whoever broke Lincoln's thumb off had to climb these ladders," she reasoned.

Marsh was busy swallowing, so he just nodded.

"And the only time it could have been done was when Stub and Ralphie were taking their coffee break," KC went on. She tapped the photo again. "This picture proves the thumb was on Lincoln's hand before their break."

Marshall swiped his tongue across his chocolatey lips. "So?"

"So maybe Stub and Ralphie saw the thieves walk between the columns but thought they were just tourists," KC said. "It would take only a few minutes for someone to climb the ladders and smack off the thumb!"

KC's eyes sparkled. "Let's go find Stub and Ralphie," she said. "If they saw the thieves, they'll be heroes!"

7
Labels and Ladders

KC called D.C. information and learned that the National Park Service had a building where they kept the maintenance equipment. It was located behind the National Museum of Natural History.

The kids trekked down Pennsylvania Avenue, then cut across a wide lawn shaded by tall trees.

The Park Service structure looked like a huge barn. It was as tall as the trees that grew around it and was built of faded bricks and thick timbers. The only entrance was a high, wide door made of wood, large enough for trucks to drive in and out. But cut into this giant-sized opening was a small, human-sized door. It, too, was closed.

Just as KC reached to knock on the door, it swung open. Two young women came out, both in gray Park Service uniforms. They each carried backpacks. "Have a good weekend, Judy," one of the women said to her friend. "See you Monday."

The women smiled at KC and Marshall. "Can we help you?" the one called Judy asked.

"We're looking for Stub and Ralphie," Marshall said.

The other woman pointed back over her shoulder. "They're in the back room," she said. "But you'd better hurry. They're getting ready to quit for the day."

KC and Marshall thanked the women and hurried inside. The floor was concrete and the room deeply shadowed. A few small light bulbs cast a dim glow from the high ceiling. The only windows were at the very top, and they were so dirty that almost no daylight came through.

The cavelike place smelled like dirt and rotting leaves. Peering into the shadows, the kids could make out large equipment for taking care of lawns and gardens. The tractors and mowers looked like sleeping monsters.

"This place is creepy," Marshall whispered. "Where are we going, anyway?"

KC pointed straight ahead at a light shining through a small door. They heard sounds coming from a radio or TV set.

When the kids reached the door, they

peeked inside. It was another massive room, but at least this one was well lit. A dusty rug lay on the concrete floor under some furniture and a TV set. On one wall, KC saw a sink. Lined up against the wall were pails, brooms, plastic buckets of soap, and a basket filled with cleaning rags.

Ralphie was sprawled on a sofa in front of the TV, eating potato chips.

Stub stood in a corner next to a ladder that leaned against the wall. High over his head, more ladders hung from a rack suspended from the ceiling.

Stub pushed a button on the wall, and a loud clanking sound drowned out the sound of the TV. The entire rack holding the ladders slowly lowered until it was level with Stub's head. When Stub released the button, the rack stopped.

"Hi," KC said. "It's KC and Marshall, remember us?"

Both men turned toward the door.

Stub blinked, then took a step toward the kids. "Oh, hi," he said. "The president's kid, right?"

KC nodded. "Well, not really, but he's my mom's husband," she said.

Ralphie sat up on the sofa.

"We're helping the president find Lincoln's thumb," KC went on. "We think it was stolen during your coffee break."

"You do?" Ralphie asked. He turned off the TV.

"It had to be then," Marshall said. He explained about the times that the two pictures were taken. "The thumb was still there when you had your picture taken at

10:07, but it was gone a half hour later."

"Yeah, you're right," Stub said. He hung the ladder on the rack, then walked over and sat in a chair.

"So is that when you went for your break?" Marshall continued.

Stub nodded. "It must've been right around then," he said. "Yeah, now I remember. That tourist who snapped my picture? I remember, we went for our break right after the guy gave Ralphie the Polaroid."

"Where were you when you drank your coffee?" KC asked. "I mean, could you see if anyone went near the statue?"

"We sat in the truck," Ralphie said.

"Yeah, but it was raining like crazy," Stub said. "I remember saying to Ralphie, 'Gee, I can't see nothing out of these windows!' So we couldn't see if anyone went near the statue or not."

"Rats!" KC said. She started pacing back and forth. She glanced at the clock on the wall. "It's almost three-thirty. The president is going to drop off the ransom in a half hour!"

"He is?" Stub asked, sitting up straighter.

"Yes, it's the only way we can get the thumb back," KC said, pacing again.

She stopped next to the rack of ladders. Behind her, she heard Marshall telling Stub and Ralphie about the ransom note.

KC had never seen so many ladders in her life. They hung straight down from the rack, like giant icicles. On the bottom rung of each ladder, there was a yellow label telling the ladder's length. Next to the yellow labels were smaller red ones with the words DANGER! KEEP AWAY FROM ELECTRIC WIRES! printed in bold black letters.

KC thought of the red mark she had seen on the stub of Lincoln's thumb. FBI scientist Pierce had told the president that the mark was some kind of red paper with glue on the back.

These labels are glued on, KC said to herself.

KC's mind raced back to ten-thirty. She and Marshall were at the statue. One of the ladders was lying on the floor where anyone could have tripped over it. Why wasn't it leaning against the statue, like the other ladder?

In her mind, she saw Stub and Ralphie

climbing the steps in front of the monument, coming from their coffee break. It was still windy, but the rain had stopped. The sun was shining.

So was Stub lying when he said it was raining during their coffee break? Why would he lie about that? Unless . . . and suddenly it all made sense to KC.

The ladder she had seen lying on the floor had knocked off the thumb. Maybe the wind had blown the ladder into the statue. When the ladder hit the thumb, part of the label scraped off, leaving the red mark.

KC felt her stomach dive toward her feet. Praying she wasn't being watched, she tried to peel off part of a red label.

"KC," she heard Marshall say.

Then she felt a hand on her shoulder.

It was Stub, and she didn't like the look on his face.

Behind Stub, Marshall looked at KC with a question in his eyes.

KC tried her best to send a silent message to Marshall: *RUN!*

Stub put a finger on the wall button. With a tremendous clatter, the ladder rack began heading toward the ceiling.

Stub turned KC toward Marshall and Ralphie. "Go have a seat next to your pal, missy," he said. "Nice and slow. Ralphie, lock the door."

8

Who Broke Lincoln's Thumb?

KC had no choice but to do as Stub told her. Her legs were shaking so hard she wasn't sure she could make it to the sofa.

"What's going on?" Marshall asked as he watched Ralphie snap the lock on the door. "Hey, why are you—"

"*They* took the thumb, Marsh," KC said. Even her voice was shaking. "These are the crooks!"

"When did you figure it out?" Stub asked, plopping into his chair.

"Just now," KC said. "When I saw those red labels on all the ladders. You left both

71

ladders standing against the statue when you took your break. You lied about it being rainy, but it was real windy. One of the ladders blew against Lincoln's hand and busted the thumb off. The red label left the red mark."

Ralphie came and sat next to Stub. "We didn't mean to break the thing off," he said. "After it happened, we didn't know what to do, so we hid it."

"Shut up, Ralphie. No one will believe it was an accident," Stub whined.

"Yeah, especially since you sent a ransom note for a hundred thousand bucks!" Marshall blurted out. "Was *that* an accident, too?"

Stub grinned. "We figured we might as well make some money." He chuckled. "Why shouldn't we get a reward for returning the famous Lincoln thumb?"

"You don't deserve any reward!" KC said, steaming. "You should've told the truth about what happened, not tried to cheat the government!"

"Besides, where is the thumb?" Marshall added. "How do we know you really have it?"

"Oh, we have it, all right," Stub said. He walked over to the wall, picked up one of the buckets, and brought it over to where the others were sitting. Then he dumped the bucket's contents onto the sofa.

What fell out was Lincoln's thumb.

KC and Marshall just stared. The marble thumb was long, smooth, and nearly white. The thumbnail was almost as big as KC's fist. The other end, where the thumb had broken, was jagged.

"What are you going to do with it?" KC asked.

Stub put the thumb back in the bucket. "First, we're gonna collect our money," he said, winking at Ralphie. "Then we'll disappear. They'll be so happy to get the thumb back, they won't even look for us."

"What about us?" Marshall asked.

The two men walked toward the door. "You'll be fine," Stub said. "The crew comes back Monday morning. You two can watch TV till then."

"Monday!" Marshall yelled. "You can't leave us till then! We'll starve!"

Ralphie pointed to his potato chips. "You can finish those," he said, unlocking the door. Both men walked out. Then KC and Marshall heard the lock click.

KC jumped up and tried to open the door, but it was solidly shut. She rattled the handle and tugged, but nothing happened.

KC took out her Swiss Army knife. She opened the sharpest blade and began hacking at the wood around the lock.

"It's no use," Marshall told her. "It will take you hours. And even if we get out of this room, we'll still be locked in the building!"

"You're right," KC admitted. She put her knife back in her pocket and flopped down on the sofa. "They're gonna get the money, and maybe they won't even leave the thumb!"

Marshall sat next to KC and picked up the bag of chips. He popped a few into his mouth. "Why aren't there any windows in this stupid building?" he mumbled.

"There are, but they're too high up," KC said. She pointed to the small windows right under the ceiling. They were about twenty feet off the floor.

Marshall looked up and nearly choked on his chips. "Ladders!" he yelled. "There are about a million of them hanging on that rack!"

Both kids flew off the sofa and ran over to the button that controlled the rack. KC pushed it, and the rack began to lower, making a terrible clatter all the way down.

"We need the tallest ladder," Marshall said.

"That one!" KC said, pointing to an aluminum ladder that looked about ten feet long. The yellow label said TWENTY FEET WHEN FULLY EXTENDED.

But when they tried to get the ladder off the rack, they couldn't budge it even an inch.

"It's too heavy," Marshall said. "We'll never get it down."

KC kicked the wall. "This is so stupid!" she shouted. "We're locked in a room full of ladders, but we can't use them!"

She reached for the button to send the ladder rack back up to the ceiling.

"Wait a sec," Marshall said. He stared at the windows high up on the wall. "I have an idea. Climb one of these ladders to the top of the rack and lie flat. I'll push the button, then climb up there with you. The rack will—"

"Take us up to the windows!" KC interrupted. "Marshall Li, you are a genius!"

Marshall blushed.

KC climbed one of the ladders until she reached the top of the rack. She got down on her stomach. The ladder ends poked into her, like rocks under a beach blanket. "Okay, now you come up," she said to Marshall.

Marshall pushed the button to raise the rack, then stopped it.

"Why'd you do that?" KC asked, gazing down at Marshall.

"We might need this," Marshall said, grabbing a small shovel off the wall. Then he mashed the button again and started climbing a ladder.

The rack clattered as it took KC and Marshall toward the ceiling of the maintenance building. Both kids were on their stomachs.

"If this thing goes too high, we're

gonna get smushed against the ceiling!" KC said. She turned her head to look up. The ceiling was only a few feet above her back, and the rack was still rising!

Suddenly the rack shook, made a final clatter, and shuddered to a stop. The kids rolled over onto their backs. Their faces were only inches from the ceiling.

Both kids had sweat dripping from their hair into their faces. "It must be two hundred degrees up here!" Marshall said. He used his T-shirt to wipe his eyes.

"Look," KC said, letting out the breath she'd been holding. Two feet away from where they perched on the rack was a small window. It was covered with soot and spiderwebs. Dead flies hung in the webs.

"Cool!" Marshall said. "I wonder where the spider is."

"Marsh, we've got a little situation here," KC said. "Can you think about spiders *after* we get out of here?"

"No problem," Marshall said. He handed KC the shovel he'd brought up, then reached over and tried to push the window out. It didn't move. Then he tried to pull the window up, but that didn't work, either.

"It's totally stuck," Marshall said. "It won't open."

"Oh yeah?" KC said. Swinging the shovel handle like a baseball bat, she smashed the blade into the filthy glass. She and Marshall covered their eyes as the window shattered and a cool breeze blew into their faces.

9

The Capture and the Cake

"Awesome!" Marshall said. He took the shovel from KC and tapped out small shards of glass still in the window's frame. When there were no more sharp edges, he leaned over and stuck out his head.

"What do you see?" KC asked.

"We're about a million miles up," Marshall said. "And that's the good news."

"What's the bad news?" KC asked.

"There's no roof under the window," Marshall said. "We can't climb out because there's nothing to stand on!"

KC just stared at Marshall. Then she wriggled to the edge of the rack and stuck her head out the window. She saw the Washington Monument in the distance. She saw the roofs of buildings and looked into the branches of trees.

And she saw tourists walking among those trees, as small as action figures.

KC took a deep breath and started screaming. "HELP! WE'RE UP HERE! LOOK, WE'RE UP HERE!"

A few of the tiny tourists stopped and looked up. KC waved down at them.

"CALL THE POLICE!" KC yelled.

One of the tourists pulled out a phone.

KC, her mother, and Marshall watched President Thornton climb the steps in front of the Lincoln Memorial. Hundreds of people stood or sat on the lawn.

The president smiled as he stepped up

to the podium. Behind him, Abraham Lincoln sat on his giant chair. He seemed to be listening, too.

And he had both thumbs.

An hour after KC and Marshall had been rescued from the maintenance building, Stub and Ralphie were arrested. They had the hundred thousand dollars with them, as well as the thumb.

"So how did they get the thumb back on Lincoln's hand so fast?" Marshall whispered to KC. "Superglue?"

"No, superwire," KC said. "They have it tied on until they can get a marble expert to fasten it on permanently."

". . . Daniel Chester French will long be remembered for this monumental achievement," the president said. "But I'm guessing he also liked to have fun. If he

were here, he'd want the party to begin!"

The crowd whistled and clapped. Red, white, and blue balloons were released and soared into the air. The United States Marine Band began playing a march.

"Let's eat!" Marshall said, grabbing KC by the arm.

Tables of food had been set up along one side of the Reflecting Pool. Marshall headed for the cake. It was about ten feet long. Blue-frosting stars decorated the corners. The rest of the cake had huge pictures of the Lincoln statue and Daniel Chester French in thick frosting.

A woman stood behind the table with a knife in her hand. "Can I cut you a piece of cake?" she asked, smiling at Marshall.

Marshall nudged KC. "Yes please," he said. "Cut me off Lincoln's left thumb!"

Did you know?

Did you know that Abraham Lincoln was the tallest president? He was six feet, four inches tall. He had an ax scar on his thumb, a mole on his cheek, and another scar over his right eye. He was the first president to have a beard while in office. He grew it because an eleven-year-old girl suggested it.

Lincoln had four sons. Sadly, three of them died when they were still boys.

The statue in the Lincoln Memorial was originally supposed to be made of bronze and twelve feet high. But the planners thought that was too small for the building. So Daniel Chester French and his workers

built a much larger statue. It is nineteen feet high and carved from twenty-eight blocks of white marble. The statue weighs 120 tons—that's 240,000 pounds! It took four years to complete.

On the statue, Lincoln's hands seem to form the sign-language letters *A* for *Abraham* and *L* for *Lincoln*. No one is sure whether French did that on purpose.

About the Author

Ron Roy is the author of more than fifty books for children, including the bestselling A to Z Mysteries® and the Capital Mysteries series. He lives in an old farmhouse in Connecticut with his dog, Pal. When he's not writing about his favorite kids in Green Lawn, Connecticut, and Washington, D.C., Ron spends time restoring his house, gardening, and traveling all over the country.